D0359539

6

THE CASE OF THE
Missing Moose

by Lewis B. Montgomery
illustrated by Amy Wummer

The KANE PRESS
New York

Library of Congress Cataloging-in-Publication Data

Montgomery, Lewis B.
The case of the missing moose / by Lewis B. Montgomery ;
illustrated by Amy Wummer.
p. cm. — (The Milo & Jazz mysteries ; 6)
Summary: While Milo and Jazz, detectives-in-training, are at summer camps on
the same lake, the mascot built by Milo's team for the color wars disappears.
ISBN 978-1-57565-331-0 (library binding) — ISBN 978-1-57565-322-8 (pbk.)
[1. Mystery and detective stories. 2. Camps—Fiction. 3. Competition (Psychology)—
Fiction. 4. Lost and found possessions—Fiction.] I. Wummer, Amy, ill. II. Title.

PZ7.M7682Cam 2011
[Fic]—dc22
2010023478

1 3 5 7 9 10 8 6 4 2

First published in the United States of America in 2011 by Kane Press, Inc.
Printed in the United States of America
WOZ0111

Book Design: Edward Miller

The Milo & Jazz Mysteries is a registered trademark of Kane Press, Inc.

www.kanepress.com

For the students and staff of

Kutztown Elementary School

—L.B.M.

CHAPTER ONE

Milo spotted the sparkly purple envelope as soon as he walked into the camp post office. A note from Jazz!

Picking it up, he felt a twinge of guilt. He remembered Jazz waving to him from the bus. "Write to me!" she had yelled. Then the bus had pulled out, taking the girls to their own camp across the lake.

That was three days ago. Since then, Jazz had written him three letters. And he had written . . . zero.

It wasn't that he didn't think of Jazz. But each time he sat down to write to her, something else came up. And the week of camp was going by so fast!

He tore open the envelope and read:

Dear Milo,

I hope you're having fun. I sure am! Camp is even better than I remembered. The girls in my cabin are all super nice, especially Olivia, my bunkmate. I told you about her, right? She's new this year, like you. She's kind of shy, but—

"Ooh! Look who got a letter from his *girlfriend*!" A hand reached out to grab the note.

Milo snatched it away just in time. He glared at the boy in the red baseball cap

and fought the urge to pull the cap down
over the boy's smirking face.

"She's not my girlfriend, Tony.
She's . . ." Milo paused. Jazz wasn't just a
friend. She was Milo's partner and fellow
sleuth. Together, they solved mysteries—
with a little help from world-famous
private eye Dash Marlowe, who mailed
them lessons. Dash had even sent them

a detective kit, with special spy glasses, a notebook, and a pair of invisible-ink pens.

But telling Tony all that wouldn't do any good. Somehow he'd find a way to make even sleuthing seem silly.

Milo felt a tug on his arm. It was his bunkmate, Gabe.

"Come on," Gabe said. "Let's get out of here."

Milo shoved Jazz's note into his pocket and followed Gabe out. They headed toward the wide lake that split the boys' camp from the girls'.

"What is Tony's problem?" Milo grumbled.

"He's just like that," Gabe said. "Always giving the new campers a hard time. Don't let him get to you."

Easy for Gabe to say, Milo thought. Tony wasn't sticking his pointy nose into everything *Gabe* did.

Milo had hardly gotten off the bus when Tony started making fun of him. Milo had never been to camp before. How was he supposed to know that the "mess hall" was where they ate? Or that "bug juice" meant cherry punch?

Except for Tony, camp was great. Milo loved everything: Nature hikes in the woods. Learning to paddle a canoe. Even jumping off the dock into the chilly lake was fun . . . well, sort of.

And color war was coming up, though no one knew exactly when. Gabe said that the breakout was always a big surprise. But the week was already half over, and—

"Hey, what's that?" Gabe pointed.

Milo looked. Near the water's edge, something stuck out. It looked like . . . an antler?

Milo ran toward it. He reached out—

"NO! DON'T TOUCH IT!" a voice shouted.

Milo's feet slid out from under him. *Splat!*

He struggled to peel himself up out of the mud.

A boy from their cabin, Wendell, rushed over clutching a camcorder. "You'll scare it away!"

Milo gaped at him. "Scare *what* away?"

Wendell flung an arm out at the water. The antler thing had shifted.

"What do you think?" he exclaimed. "The lake moose!"

CHAPTER TWO

Lake moose?

"Nobody's ever seen it come ashore!" Wendell went on. "And nobody has ever captured it on video! I'll be the first to—"

"Let me see that." Gabe squished past him, grabbed the thing sticking out of the water, and yanked it free. He waved it in the air. "Sorry, Wendell. No lake moose."

Wendell's face fell. Then he brightened. "But we found its antlers!"

"I think it's just a piece of driftwood," Gabe said, rubbing off the mud.

Looking closer, Milo realized Gabe was right. But it really did look like the antlers of a moose.

Wendell didn't seem to hear Gabe. Taking the driftwood, he turned it over in his hands. "Where are you, lake moose?" he muttered.

Clang! The bell rang for dinner. Leaving Wendell gazing out at the lake, Milo and Gabe headed to the mess hall.

"What does he mean, 'lake moose'?" Milo asked.

Gabe shot him a sideways glance. "Nobody told you yet about the giant moose that lives deep in the middle of the lake?"

Milo shook his head.

"They say it's got flippers for feet,"

Gabe said, "and teeth just like a shark." He lowered his voice. "You know what else I heard? Once, years and years ago, two boys went out in a canoe at night . . . and they *never came back.*"

Milo swallowed. "You mean . . ."

Gabe nodded solemnly. "The lake moose got 'em."

"You're kidding, right?" Milo asked. "There isn't really any such thing as a lake moose . . . is there?"

His friend shrugged. "Maybe not. Still, I've never heard of anyone paddling all the way across the lake."

"Has anybody actually seen it?"

"Some of the older boys say they did. But I think they're making it up."

Had Jazz heard about the lake moose? Milo wondered. He pictured her eyebrow going up. Jazz really didn't believe in spooky stuff like that.

Neither do I! he reminded himself quickly. Still . . .

Gabe went into the mess hall. Milo hosed the mud off his hands and knees, but his T-shirt was a lost cause.

Inside, he joined the dinner line and read the rest of Jazz's note.

> . . . She's new this year, like you. She's kind of shy, but nice. She's got a brother who sounds just as bad as Chris!

Milo grinned. Jazz always complained about her three older siblings. *She should try living with a little brother*, he thought. Actually, he almost missed Ethan. . . .

> See you at the bus on Saturday! Write back!   —J

It felt funny knowing Jazz was right across the lake, but not getting to see or talk to her. At least he'd made a friend in his cabin. He headed over to join Gabe.

As he passed the table where Tony sat with his cabin mates, Tony called to him. "Hey! Want to hear a dirty joke?"

Before he could answer, Tony pointed at Milo's muddy shirt. "It's—*you*!"

Tony and his friends guffawed.

Milo's face grew hot. He turned away. Why couldn't Tony just leave him alone?

While the campers ate their dinner, the head counselor, Dan, stood to speak. Milo half listened as Dan went on about water safety and talking after lights-out.

Suddenly Milo noticed an odd tapping sound. He looked down the table. Frankie, his own counselor, was drumming with his fork and knife.

Dan raised his voice.

Frankie started making beatbox sounds. *Puh-ch. Puh-puh-ch. Tsss—*

Snickers rose around the mess hall. Milo tried to catch Gabe's eye. What in the world was Frankie doing? Counselors didn't act this way.

Dan stopped mid-sentence. "Frankie!"

"Yeah?"

Folding his arms, Dan asked grimly, "Am I boring you?"

Milo waited for Frankie to apologize. Instead, his counselor nodded. "Yeah. You're boring everybody."

Gasps flew around the mess hall.

Storming over, Dan shouted, "Take it back!"

Frankie stood up. "Make me."

Dan scowled. His gaze darted around. It landed on a plastic ketchup bottle.

"You wouldn't," Frankie said.

Dan smiled. "Wouldn't I?"

Then he picked up the ketchup bottle, aimed, and squeezed.

CHAPTER THREE

A hush fell over the hall. Milo stared at
his counselor. Wow! Frankie was a mess!

Frankie stared down at himself,
too. He looked at Dan. He looked at
the table. Then, in one swift move, he
grabbed his plate and dumped his meal
over Dan's head.

Dan shook his head like an angry
lion. Bits of food flew off. "You know
what this means?" he roared. "This
means— This means—"

Milo held his breath. He liked Frankie. What was going to happen next?

"This means . . . *WAR!*"

Suddenly, pandemonium broke out. All the counselors yelled, "Color war!" and flung red and blue papers into the air. Smiling now, Dan and Frankie gave each other a high five. Campers laughed and shouted, grabbing at the sheets of paper as they fluttered down.

Milo snatched a paper from the floor and read: ALL ABOUT COLOR WAR. There were three cabins on each team. Milo and Gabe's cabin was on the blue team. Tony's cabin was on the red.

He skimmed over the list of events. Flag football, relay races, tug-of-war . . . Color war was going to be great!

Someone bumped into him hard, nearly knocking him down.

It was Tony.

"Feeling blue yet?" Tony taunted. "You will soon! Red team is gonna stomp all over you!"

Whirling his cap over his head, Tony ran off.

Milo wondered what Tony would have done if he'd ended up on the blue team. He wore that red cap every day. He probably even wore it to bed.

Back at the cabin, all anyone could talk about was color war. Everyone loved the surprise breakout, though a few boys who had been at camp before swore they knew Frankie and Dan were faking all along.

Frankie passed out blue T-shirts.

"Okay, guys, listen up," he told them. "The final event of color war will be the bonfire two nights from now."

"The bonfire is awesome!" Gabe whispered to Milo.

Frankie went on, "For the bonfire, each team needs to come up with three things—a cheer, a mascot, and a flag. These count for *major* points. Our cabin gets to make the blue team's mascot—"

An excited buzz went up.

"Grizzly bear!" a boy yelled out.

Gabe shook his head. "The red team did that last year."

Another boy said, "Something blue?"

"Blue jay!"

"Nah."

Milo glanced across the cabin.
Wendell was sitting on his cot filming the
driftwood "antlers" with his camcorder.
He didn't seem to notice what was going
on around him.

"It should be fierce," somebody said.
"To scare the other team."

Hmm. *Fierce and scary*, Milo thought.
His glance landed on Wendell again.

Hey!

He jumped up. "How about a moose?
The lake moose?"

Gabe caught on right away. "Yeah! We
could use those antlers—"

"Antlers?" Frankie asked.

Milo pointed. "That driftwood.
Doesn't it look a lot like moose antlers?
We found it at the lake."

All eyes turned to Wendell's cot.

Wendell glanced up. "Huh?"

Patiently, Gabe explained their plan.

"Use the lake moose for a *mascot*?"
Wendell looked horrified. "What if it
finds out?"

The other boys burst out laughing.

"Come on, Wendell!"

"Don't be such a goof."

Wendell gazed around the cabin.
Finally he shrugged. "Okay. Fine."

Gabe clapped Milo on the shoulder.
"This will be the greatest mascot ever!"

As the rest of his cabin mates
cheered, Milo's eyes met Wendell's.

Wendell did not look happy.

Not happy at all.

CHAPTER FOUR

At breakfast, the blue team sat on one side of the mess hall. The red team sat on the other.

"You all know that winning events will help your team," Dan told them. "But you can gain or lose points other ways, too. By being good or bad sports. Being on time, or late—"

"And neatness counts," Frankie put in. "So let's see which side of this mess hall can get cleaned up fas—"

Scraping benches drowned him out as the two teams rushed to clear their tables. Color war was on!

Milo's first event was a swim race. As he swam out to the marker, his mind flashed to the lake moose. *Teeth just like a shark . . .*

Tagging the marker, he turned back. Just then, something brushed against his toes.

Heart racing, he put on a burst of speed. He was gasping for breath as he reached the dock. Gabe stuck out a hand to haul him up. "Third place! All right!"

Milo glanced back out at the lake. Nothing. His foot had just touched a floating weed or something . . . right?

The boys changed out of their wet swim trunks, then ran to the big field for flag football. Milo fumbled a pass, but Gabe picked up the ball and scored a touchdown for a blue team win.

After lunch, Milo and his cabin mates stopped at the arts-and-crafts hut. Loaded down with moose-making supplies, they rushed back to the cabin and got to work.

Only Wendell didn't seem excited. Twice, Milo saw him shooting glances at his camcorder. Still, Wendell pitched in with the others.

When the bell rang, the boys groaned.

"Can't we be a little late to dinner?" Milo begged. "We're almost done."

To their amazement, Frankie brought them their food from the mess hall. It was pizza night, and they all munched happily as they worked.

Milo paused to admire the moose. Its pasteboard teeth were perfect—sharp and scary. Its flippers were a little floppy, but not too bad. And the antlers . . . *wow*!

No way could the red team ever come up with anything as cool as this. He couldn't wait to see their faces at the bonfire tomorrow night.

The boys finished just before dusk.

They left their moose to dry and hurried
out to the big field for the sunset relays.

For the first relay, they lined up and
passed a dripping sponge over their heads,
racing to get it to the end of the line. Soon
they were all soaked and laughing.

Next came the three-legged race, then a race with paper plates of shaving cream balanced on their heads.

The "hen race" was the silliest of all. They waddled with a raw egg between their knees, then "laid" it in a box and squawked.

Milo's team wasn't doing very well. But he was having so much fun, he didn't mind.

The only thing that spoiled it was Tony. He took every chance to bump into Milo or try to trip him. In the balloon race, he even popped Milo's balloon.

"Hey!" Milo protested.

Sneering, Tony stuck his pointy nose right in Milo's face. "What are you going to do about it, blue boy?"

Milo wished he could think of a crushing comeback, the way Jazz would. Instead, he just turned away.

When the relay races ended, the boys straggled off to bed, tired but happy.

As they came up to their cabin, Gabe slung an arm across Milo's shoulder. "Man, you looked great laying that egg. Sure you're not a chicken?"

Milo pushed open the screen door and flipped the light on. "Very fun—"

His grin froze as he stared at the empty space in the middle of the cabin.

The lake moose was gone.

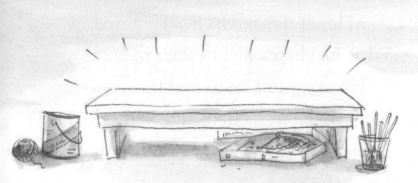

CHAPTER FIVE

The boys crowded into the cabin.

"Oh, no!"

"I don't believe it!"

"How—?"

Frankie came in. They clustered around him, all shouting at once.

Their counselor shook his head. "Okay, guys. I'm going to tell Dan."

He walked out.

Milo sat down. His head whirled. What had happened to their mascot?

It was up to him to find the answer. After all, he was a detective, wasn't he? But he had never tackled a case without Jazz before. . . .

His cabin mates were slumped on their bunks. One of them grumbled, "How are we going to beat the red team without our mascot?"

Of course! Milo jumped up.

"I think someone from the red team stole the mascot!" he exclaimed. "To lose us points."

Silence.

"Duh," someone said.

Milo looked around at his cabin mates. "You . . . you knew?"

Gabe patted his shoulder. "Milo, this is color war."

"You should have seen last year's canoe race," a boy said. "The blue team switched the red team's canoe with that old leaky one—"

"Good thing they had life jackets," someone else chimed in.

"Yeah, but they sure got wet."

"You should have seen their faces when their boat started to sink!"

"How about the blue team's faces when Dan made them swap canoes and race again?"

"And then there was the time the red

team stole the blue team's flag and flew it from the top of the latrine. . . ."

Everyone laughed.

Milo shook his head. "I don't get it. You mean that stuff is *allowed*?"

"Oh, no. It drives the counselors nuts," Gabe said. "Still, it happens."

"But what about our moose mascot?" Milo asked. "We worked so hard!"

"The counselors will get it back," Gabe promised.

But Frankie returned empty-handed. He said they had searched all the cabins and every other building in the camp. No sign of their lake moose.

It still hadn't turned up in the morning. At breakfast, Dan gave a stern lecture, demanding the return of the blue team's mascot. Nobody stepped forward.

"We've got to figure out where they hid the moose!" Milo told Gabe as they left the mess hall. "Tonight's the bonfire. We can't show up without a mascot."

Gabe frowned. "We could try to make another one. . . ."

"With what? A lake moose wouldn't be a lake moose without antlers. And that piece of driftwood was one-of-a-kind."

"It'll turn up," Gabe said. But he looked worried.

Leaving Gabe at the cabin, Milo went to check his mail. There was another sparkly purple note, reminding him he still hadn't written to Jazz.

He also had a letter from his parents. When he opened it, he found a second envelope inside. The upper left-hand corner said *DM*.

A new detective lesson from Dash Marlowe!

Before he could tear it open, someone came into the office. *Tony.*

Milo jammed the mail into his pocket to read later. He was in no mood for girlfriend jokes.

But Tony had something else in mind.

"I hear you lost your moosie toy. Aw." He made a sad face. "Now you can't get to sleep at night."

Milo boiled over. "It's our mascot! And it's going to win us color war . . ."

Tony smirked. "If you find it in time."

"We will." But his voice wobbled.

Tony's smile widened.

"Oh, I don't think so, blue boy. In fact,
I don't think you'll find it at all. Ever."

CHAPTER SIX

"Tony really said that?" Gabe asked. They were sitting on the cabin steps, painting Gabe's face blue.

Milo nodded.

"What did you say?"

"I said, 'How would you know?'"

"And?" Gabe pressed.

"And he laughed and walked away."

Milo dabbed a streak of paint on his friend's forehead. "Tony stole our mascot, Gabe. I know it. He practically told me so."

"Sure sounds like it," Gabe agreed. "While we were all out at the relay races, he must have gone off and . . ."

Milo interrupted. "Relay races?"

Gabe gave him a funny look. "Uh-huh. Last night. The sunset relays. Remember? That was the only time we left the moose alone."

"But Tony never left the sunset relays," Milo said.

"You sure?"

"I would have noticed. Believe me." Tony had been acting so obnoxious, Milo would have been thrilled to see him walk away. Puzzled, Milo scratched his head.

"Maybe he got somebody else to do it. Did you see anybody on the red team sneak away?"

"No, I—" Gabe suddenly paused.

"What? You saw someone?"

Gabe frowned. "No . . . no one on the red team." He pointed. "You've got paint in your hair."

Milo's hand flew to his head.

His friend laughed. "Now it's worse."

A group of red team boys walked by, led by a familiar figure in a baseball cap. As he sauntered past, Tony called out, "Hey, blue boy. Find your moosie yet?" His teammates snorted.

Milo watched them go. If only Jazz were here. Together they would—well, what *would* he and Jazz do? Not sit

around and watch a suspect walk away,
that was for sure.

He jumped up off the step.

"I'm going to go talk to Tony."

Gabe looked horrified. "Why?"

"To question him," Milo explained.

"He's not going to tell you anything."

Milo shrugged. "I have to try, anyway.
Maybe he'll let something slip."

"Milo . . . maybe I should tell you . . ."

Tony was moving away from them.

Milo clapped Gabe on the shoulder, leaving his T-shirt smeared with paint. "Got to go. Later, okay?"

"But—"

Milo ran.

At a picnic table near the mess hall, campers from both teams had gathered to compete at building houses out of cards. Tony and his friends were headed that way.

"Wait up!" Milo called.

Tony glanced back, but didn't seem to see him. Then, suddenly, Tony stopped. The other boys gathered around him in a huddle.

As Milo drew closer, he heard Tony say, ". . . and I'll switch the hiding spot."

The huddle broke up, and Tony ran

off toward the woods. His friends moved on without him.

Milo stood frozen in place.

The hiding spot?

No wonder the counselors hadn't been able to find the missing mascot. Tony had hidden it in the woods!

Quickly, Milo hurried down the path Tony had taken.

At first, he didn't see Tony at all. Then, through the trees, he caught a flash of red. He followed.

Milo had trailed suspects before with Jazz. But they had always been in town. It was different out in the woods.

Twigs snapped. Dry leaves crunched. Once, Tony turned as if he heard him. But then he walked on.

Milo hung further back. That made it hard to keep Tony in sight. Twice, he almost lost him.

Sweat dripped down the back of Milo's neck. He hardly noticed. They must be getting close. Any second now, they'd reach the hiding place.

Milo pictured himself marching into camp in triumph with the missing moose. He could almost hear his team's cheers. He'd be a hero.

Wait . . . where was Tony?

Milo turned in circles, searching for a glimpse of red. But all he saw was the green and brown of the woods.

He stood very still, listening for the crunch of feet. But all he heard was a mosquito buzzing.

Suddenly, he realized he had no idea where he was. His only thought had been to follow Tony. He hadn't paid attention to where they were going.

He was lost.

CHAPTER SEVEN

Milo's heart thumped.

On the first day of camp, they had been told what to do if they ever got lost: Stay calm. Stay put. Call for help.

Okay.

A jet plane passed high overhead. Milo waved his arms. "HEY! DOWN HERE! HEY! *HEY!*"

The plane kept going.

What was it Frankie had said to do? Spell out HELP with rocks or sticks. . . .

Milo was just finishing the *H* when a voice said, "There you are!"

He jumped.

"Gabe!" He rushed toward his friend. "How did you find me?"

"I saw Tony come out of the woods, and then I heard you yelling."

"Heard me? All the way from camp?" Milo asked.

"I was just right over there," Gabe said. "Watching the card house contest." Milo followed his pointing finger. Above the trees, something gleamed in the sun: the mess-hall roof.

He hadn't been lost deep in the woods. Tony must have led him in circles!

Gabe looked at the *H* on the ground.

"What are you doing?"

Hastily, Milo kicked it apart. "Oh, nothing."

When they came out of the woods, Milo saw Tony sitting with his friends. As soon as they saw Milo, they all burst out laughing.

"Hey, blue boy," Tony called out. "Been for a nice walk? *Find* anything?"

Milo's face burned. What kind of a sleuth was he, to let a suspect lead him on a—well, on a wild *moose* chase?

"Did you get anything out of Tony?" Gabe asked as they walked off.

"No," Milo said gloomily.

Gabe shook his head. "Listen, Milo. I'm not so sure Tony took the mascot."

"But he said—"

"Maybe he just said that stuff to make you feel bad."

"Well, who do you think stole it?" Milo asked.

Slowly, Gabe said, "You know how you were asking me if I saw anybody sneak away during the sunset relays? Well, I did see someone."

"Who?"

Gabe looked miserable. "Wendell."

"*Wendell?*" Milo repeated.

His friend nodded.

"But he's on the blue team with us!" Milo said. "He's in our cabin! He even helped us make the moose!"

"I know, I know!" Gabe said. "Still . . . he didn't seem so happy about it, did he?"

Milo's mind raced. Gabe was right. Wendell hadn't wanted them to make a lake moose mascot. Wendell was afraid the real lake moose would be mad.

What if Wendell had stolen the mascot? What if he had done something crazy—like thrown it in the lake?

Leaving Gabe behind, Milo rushed off.

He found Wendell alone in their cabin playing with his camcorder.

"Where's the mascot?" Milo demanded.

Wendell glanced up. "Huh?"

"You came back here during the relay races and stole the mascot!" Milo said.

Wendell looked shocked. "I did not!"

"Gabe saw you go."

"I left the races," Wendell said, "but I didn't come here. I went to the lake."

"The lake? At night?"

"Sure. That's when the lake moose is supposed to come out." Wendell waved his camcorder. "I wanted to be ready."

Now Milo didn't know *what* to think. Wendell sounded sincere. Was he telling the truth?

"I'll show you." Eagerly, Wendell pushed buttons on the camcorder. "See? There's the lake." Fast-forwarding, he pointed to the tiny clock on the screen. "After I left the relay races, I was there for the whole time."

So Wendell hadn't stolen the moose after all. But then . . . who had?

Something red zipped across the camcorder screen.

"Wait! What was that?" Milo asked.

"Not the lake moose," Wendell told him sadly. "It never showed."

"Back it up!" Milo said. "Please!"

Shrugging, Wendell obeyed.

Milo stared at the camcorder screen. That baseball hat. That pointy nose.

"It's *Tony*!"

CHAPTER EIGHT

Wendell peered over Milo's shoulder.
"Oh, yeah. I guess I did see him go by.
But he got out of my way pretty fast."

Milo grabbed the camcorder.

"Hey!" Wendell grabbed it back.

"I need to borrow it," Milo begged.
"Just for a little while."

Frowning, Wendell slowly let it go.
Milo dashed away.

The card house contest had ended. Tony and his friends were gone. Near the empty picnic table, Milo spotted Gabe.

"Gabe! It wasn't Wendell after all! Tony did sneak off from the races last night!" He waved the camcorder. "Look!"

Quickly, he ran the video for Gabe, who nodded. "That's Tony, all right. I guess you didn't have your eye on him the *whole* time."

"But I did!" Milo stopped, confused. There was no way Tony could have left the sunset relays without him noticing. And yet . . . he'd been down by the lake. The video was proof.

How could Tony have been in two places at once?

Frustrated, Milo took the camcorder

and trudged back toward the cabin. He was no closer to finding the missing mascot than when he started—and soon it would be time for the bonfire.

The red team was way ahead in points. Without the mascot, there was practically no chance the blue team could catch up and win. He had failed.

Finding the cabin empty, Milo flopped onto his bunk. His pocket crackled, reminding him that he had stuffed his unread mail in it earlier.

He pulled out the lesson from Dash and the note from Jazz. He opened Dash's lesson first. Maybe it would help him with his case.

Communication

Sleuths know how to keep the wrong people from picking up our messages: Hidden drop-off spots. Secret codes. Invisible-ink pens.

But sometimes we need to make sure that the right person *does* get the message. When you're working with a partner, nothing matters more than good communication.

I learned that as a sleuth-in-training with the legendary detective Madame X. On the trail of a rare-animal thief, we went to a banquet at the zoo. While the wealthy guests nibbled canapés and showed off their own fur and feathers—fake, of course!—we mingled with the crowd and searched for clues.

Madame X appeared at my elbow. "I've found the thief!" she whispered. "Keep an eye on the boa while I go for the police." And she slipped away.

I rushed to the snake house, but found no one there. The giant boa constrictor stared back at me from behind the glass, its forked tongue flicking in and out. Then, suddenly, it turned and vanished into the back of its cage.

Nervously, I peered through the glass. Could the thief have broken in through the back door to the cage? Even now, was the huge boa slithering out to

"AAAAAAAHHHHH!" I screamed, as something wrapped around my arm and squeezed.

It was Madame X.

"What in the world are you doing?" she asked angrily. "While you've been wandering around the zoo, the thief got away."

"But you told me to keep an eye on the boa!" I protested.

Madame X groaned. "Oh, Dash! The thief was the woman in the *feather* boa."

Rubbing my arm, I turned back to the cage. The boa constrictor had come out again, and it flicked its tongue at me. If I didn't know better, I'd have sworn it was laughing.

So when you need to communicate, make sure your partner gets the message. Be clear. Be complete. And remember: people can't read minds. (Well, there *was* The Case of the Clairvoyant Crook—but that's another story. . . .)

Dropping Dash's letter, Milo sighed. Jazz wasn't even with him on this case. Good communication wasn't going to solve anything.

He opened Jazz's note.

How come you haven't written back?
Too busy with color war? Our color war
breakout was fantastic. They woke us
up in the middle of the night and gave
out green and yellow cupcakes!

Olivia and I won the canoe race for
the yellow team. You should have seen
the Big Banana go! (That's what we call
our canoe.)

How's your team doing?

—J

P.S.

The note ended
there. Jazz must
have gotten busy
and forgotten that
she hadn't written
her P.S. before she
sent the letter.

Milo got out a pen and paper, but he couldn't think of where to start. How could he write a cheerful note like Jazz's, when everything was going wrong?

Just as his pen touched the paper, Wendell burst into the cabin.

"I need my camcorder! Right now!"

Milo sat up. "What's going on?"

"It's the lake moose!" Wendell cried. "It's come ashore!"

CHAPTER NINE

Wendell grabbed the camcorder and rushed back out. Milo chased after him.

"The *real* lake moose?"

"What else?" Wendell asked.

As they ran down the path to the lake, Milo wasn't sure what he expected to see.

Wendell waved. "Over here!"

Milo followed him down to the shore.

Camcorder raised, Wendell was zooming in on . . . the empty ground?

"Where's the lake moose?"

Wendell glanced up. "In the lake?"

"I thought you said it came ashore!" Milo said.

"It did! And I found its tracks." Wendell pointed. "See the broken twigs? And look, where it dragged itself up, there in the mud—a belly print!"

Milo groaned and shook his head. Why did he listen to Wendell's stories? He should have known.

As he turned to leave, a flash of yellow caught his eye.

He looked a little closer at the spot Wendell had pointed out. Half-buried in the mud lay a large rock. On the rock, there was a scrape of what looked like yellow paint.

Yellow . . .

Milo looked out across the lake. Then he stared back down at the rock.

Something had come ashore, all right. But was it the lake moose? Or . . . *something else?*

Yelling, "Thanks, Wendell!" over his shoulder, he scrambled up the path. Racing into the cabin, he snatched up Jazz's note and read it through again. At the blank P.S., he stopped.

Jazz wouldn't forget to write a P.S. Jazz never forgot anything.

He was the one who forgot things— like their *invisible-ink pens.*

Hastily, he dug in his duffel bag and came up with his pen. Flipping on its special light, he shone it onto Jazz's note.

Aha!

P.S. I don't want Olivia to see this, but I'm worried about her. She's been acting so weird! Today she got a letter from her brother and she went off alone to read it. Then, during dinner, she sneaked away and didn't come back until after dark. She wouldn't tell me where she'd been but she looked pretty upset. Milo, something strange is going on.

Milo couldn't hold in his excitement. Jazz must have written the letter last night—just after the mascot disappeared.

Olivia's mysterious behavior. Strange marks by the lake. The missing moose . . .

It was all starting to make sense! Well, almost all. And he had a plan that just might work. With Jazz's help, there was a chance he could still get the blue team's mascot back and win the color war.

But he had to hurry.

Quickly, he scrawled a note to Jazz. Then he rushed to the camp post office, where a counselor from the girls' camp was picking up the mail.

Milo pressed the note into her hand. "Please, can you make sure my friend gets this right away?" he pleaded.

He heard a guffaw behind him. Tony—who else?

"Aw! A love letter. Isn't that sweet?"

Milo ignored him. For once, he couldn't care less about Tony's teasing. All he cared about was reaching Jazz.

The counselor smiled down at him. "I'll do my best."

As he left, Milo glanced at the clock. Less than three hours before the bonfire! What if Jazz didn't get the note in time? What if his plan fell through?

He thought of Dash's lesson and groaned. If only he'd been writing to Jazz all along. What a dope he'd been!

The hours ticked by slowly. By the time everyone gathered at the fire pit, Milo's stomach was in knots.

The two teams sat across from each other. They waved their flags and cheered till they were hoarse.

Tony marched up and down triumphantly, waving the red team's cardboard mascot. It was supposed to be a fox, but Milo thought it looked more like a kitten with a toilet brush for a tail.

Frankie stood up. "Since the blue team's mascot mysteriously vanished," he said, "the counselors have decided to award both mascots equal points."

Boos and grumbles came from the red team. The blue team clapped half-heartedly.

Milo jumped to his feet. "NO!"

Everybody stared at him.

"Our mascot is way better than theirs," Milo protested.

"Oh, yeah?" Tony taunted loudly. "Well, let's see it, then!"

Milo crossed his fingers.

Jazz, please don't let me down. . . .

Aloud, he just said, "Follow me."

Buzzing with curiosity, the campers and the counselors streamed after him down to the lake.

Wendell trotted up next to Milo. "You're going to make the real lake moose come out of the lake! Right? Right?"

Milo stared out at the empty lake without answering.

Boys began to murmur restlessly.
Tony sneered, "That's your mascot, huh?
A big fat nothing!"

"Milo wouldn't bring us all down here
for nothing," Gabe said loyally.

Then Wendell called out, "Look!"

A dark shape was moving across the
lake. Slowly, it came toward them, closer
and closer.

"It's the lake moose!"
Wendell cried.

Then
somebody else
shouted, "No! It's
a canoe!"

Two figures
paddled the canoe
to shore. It scraped

against the rocks, and the person in front hopped out.

"Jazz!" Milo yelled. "You made it!"

She grinned at him. "*We* made it." Then she turned and pulled a tarp off the large thing in the middle of the canoe.

"Our mascot!" Gabe shouted.

But Milo wasn't looking at the mascot. He was looking past it.

Climbing out of the canoe and sloshing forward to face Tony was . . .

Milo stared.

Another Tony?

CHAPTER TEN

Milo gaped from one Tony to the other. Same red cap. Same pointy nose. Then the Tony who had come in the canoe took off his cap and shook out his long hair.

Milo blinked. *Her* hair.

The second Tony was a girl!

"This is Olivia," Jazz said. She turned to Tony. "And you must be her twin brother. She's told me a *lot* about you."

Twins, Milo thought. *Of course!*

Tony scowled at Olivia. "What are you doing here?"

"We came to bring the mascot back," she answered.

Dan folded his arms. "And how, exactly, did the blue team's mascot end up at the girls' camp?"

Olivia looked down. "I . . . I stole it."

"You?" Gabe exclaimed. "How? *Why?*"

"Tony made me do it!" Olivia cried.

A strangled sound from Tony interrupted her. "That's not—"

Dan silenced Tony with a look. "Go on, Olivia."

"Tony said if I didn't steal the moose, he'd tell all the girls I didn't go to camp last year because I wet my bed."

A couple of boys snickered.

She turned pink. "It isn't true! I didn't go because I was too shy."

Jazz put an arm around her friend.

Olivia went on. "A little before dark last night, I paddled over—"

"*Alone?*" Dan asked.

She nodded.

The counselors traded horrified looks, while the boys said, "Wow!" and "Cool!"

Wendell's jaw hung open. "Weren't you scared of the lake moose?"

Olivia shook her head. "I don't believe that old story."

"But it's real! I saw its tracks!"

"Those weren't lake moose tracks," Milo told him. "Olivia's canoe made those marks when she pulled it ashore." He looked at Jazz. "I guessed it when I saw the yellow paint that had scraped off the underside. The Big Banana, right?"

Jazz nodded. "I showed Olivia the note you wrote me about what you suspected. She broke down and admitted everything." Jazz grinned at him. "She was amazed that you figured it out."

Milo said, "But there was one thing I couldn't figure out—how Tony could be at the sunset relays and down at the lake at the same time." He turned to Olivia. "But it was *you* Wendell caught on video last night. He thought you were Tony— and I made the same mistake."

"Tony knew everyone would notice a girl in the boys' camp," Olivia said. "So he told me to tuck my hair under my cap for a disguise."

"She's lying!" Tony burst out. "She made it all up to get me into trouble." He stared hard at Olivia. "*Didn't you?*"

Olivia shrank under her twin's glare. She shot a nervous look at Jazz.

Before Jazz could say anything, Wendell spoke up. "You can't scare Olivia!" he said. "She's brave. She crossed the lake alone! At night!"

Olivia seemed to grow taller.

"I'm telling the truth," she said. "And I can prove it. I've got Tony's letters."

Something clicked in Milo's brain. *That's why Tony was always at the camp post office. He was writing to Olivia!*

Tony's face was as red as his cap. And for once, he had nothing to say.

Dan had been whispering with the other counselors. Now he stepped forward and cleared his throat.

"Well," he said. "Adding in the points for the blue team's excellent mascot—"

"Go, Milo!" Gabe called out.

Dan went on, "And subtracting points from the red team for Tony's cheating—"

The red team booed.

"The winner of this year's color war is . . . *the blue team!*"

The blue team burst into cheers.
Glowering, Tony tore off his cap and
flung it on the ground. Then he snatched
it up and stormed away.

Dan turned to the girls. "I'll have to call your counselors to come and get you. I'm guessing they won't be too pleased."

"I'll explain that it was all my fault," Olivia promised Jazz. She looked at Milo. "I'm sorry about taking your mascot."

"I'm just glad we got it back," he said. "I hope you won't get in a lot of trouble."

Olivia glanced off in the direction her brother had gone, and she smiled a little. "That's okay. It's worth it."

Milo asked Dan, "While the girls are waiting to be picked up, can they come to the bonfire?"

Dan rubbed his chin. "Well . . . I don't see why not."

Wendell was still gazing at Olivia. "I'll toast you a marshmallow!" he said. "I'll even let you try out my camcorder."

Milo grinned at him. "You don't want to stay and watch for the lake moose?"

"Lake moose?" Wendell said vaguely as he left with Olivia. "What lake moose?"

When everyone was gone, Milo turned to Jazz. "Thanks for your help."

She smiled. "No problem, partner. That was pretty good detective work."

"I could have solved it faster," he said, "if I'd only known Tony had a twin sister at the girls' camp. . . ."

Jazz raised an eyebrow. "I could have told you that—if you'd written to me sooner."

"Next time I will," he promised. "Dash is right—nothing's more important than communicating with your partner!"

Jazz looked puzzled. "Dash said that? When? You didn't get a lesson and not tell me, did you? *Milo?*"

But Milo only half heard her. He was staring over her shoulder, out at the lake.

For an instant, he'd seen something pop out of the water. Something big, with sharp, flashing teeth. He was sure of it.

Well, *almost* sure. . . .

SUPER SLEUTHING STRATEGIES

A few days after Milo and Jazz wrote to Dash Marlowe, a letter arrived in the mail. . . .

Greetings, Milo and Jazz,
   Congratulations on solving another case! It's great you learned early in your detecting career how important it is to communicate with your partner. (I'm talking to you, Milo.) Things can really go wrong when detectives are in two different places, as I learned during The Case of the Two-Timing Travelers. *Don't* remind me to tell you about that one!

Happy Sleuthing!
—*Dash Marlowe*

Warm Up!
Here are some Brain Stretchers to work those mental muscles. (But if you make like a tree and get stumped, the answers are at the end of this letter.)

1. Two eggs are put in the same pot of water at the very same time. One takes 40 minutes to hard-boil, while the other takes only 15 minutes. Why?
2. A certain five-letter word becomes *shorter* when you add two letters to it. What is the word?
3. How was a man who had never seen his own face able to draw a picture that looked exactly like himself?
4. Three large people try to crowd under one small umbrella, but nobody gets wet. How is this possible?

Spot the Difference!

Twins can be tricky. Take Jill and Joy and Brad and Bart, below. Each pair of twins looks just alike—but if you use your detective skills and observe closely, you'll find seven differences between them!

Answer: The girl on the left has more strands of hair on her forehead, no eyebrows, more eyelashes, a barrette, no earrings, no freckles, and a beaded necklace. The girl on the right has fewer strands of hair on her forehead, one eyebrow, fewer eyelashes, no barrette, earrings, freckles, and a locket. The boy on the left has no cowlick, a curl on his forehead, one short eyebrow, a dimple by his mouth, no missing teeth, no bandage on his neck, and a V-neck shirt. The boy on the right has a cowlick, no curl on his forehead, two full eyebrows, no dimple by his mouth, a missing tooth, a bandage on his neck, and a crew-neck shirt.

Mail Call: A Logic Puzzle

Three ex-robbers loved getting mail when they were in prison. But what was each guy's favorite and least favorite kind of mail? Look at the clues and fill in the answer box where you can. Then read the clues again to find the answer.

1. The ex-robber who dreamed of faraway places was not Rocky.
2. Louie loved Valentine's Day cards, especially from his mom.
3. The robber who couldn't stand Valentine's Day was head over heels for lessons by mail.
4. Louie hated to get travel advertising unless it was for somewhere he didn't want to go, like Guam.
5. Rocky thought hearts were stupid.

	Rocky	Louie	Sal
Best Mail			
Worst Mail			

Answer: Louie loved Valentines but travel ads got on his nerves. Rocky didn't care for Valentines but loved the idea of learning new things. Sal wasn't into learning but went gaga over travel ads.

92

The Message: A Mini-Mystery

Here's the story of a victim who tried very hard to communicate—and almost failed.

Dan Lee, the senior partner at Kannalla, Long, and Lee, called me to his office. He seemed groggy and very upset. Working late the night before, he had been drugged and his cash box was stolen. He was found the next day slumped over his computer, unable to remember what had happened but sure that his attacker had been someone he knew.

Luckily, Lee had left one clue. Before he passed out he had typed something on his computer: Iqhhqooq. The police said it was nonsense and meant nothing. "But it does mean something," Lee told me. "I was trying to type a message—I know it!" I looked at the computer keyboard and smiled. "Of course it means something," I said. "You typed the name of the man who drugged and robbed you."

So how did I draw that conclusion—and solve the mystery?

Answer: Lee's partner, Kannalla, was the robber. First I noticed there were eight letters in the word on Lee's computer screen—and eight letters in Kannalla's name. Then it hit me. Good typists always start with their fingers on the middle row of keys—the letters a-s-d-f and j-k-l. But Lee, drugged and confused, put his fingers on the higher row of letters instead. So when he tried to type "Kannalla", he typed I instead of K, q instead of a and so forth.

93

Headline Howlers: A Communication Puzzle

Talk about a failure to communicate! The headlines below (from actual newspapers!) can be read in two totally different ways. See if you can figure out both what the headline was supposed to mean and the funny meaning that sneaked in by accident.

1. POLICE FOUND SAFE UNDER BED
2. COW INJURES FARMER WITH AX
3. KIDS MAKE NUTRITIOUS SNACKS
4. HOSPITALS ARE SUED BY 7 FOOT DOCTORS
5. DEALERS WILL HEAR CAR TALK AT NOON
6. STOLEN PAINTING FOUND BY TREE

Answers: 1. The police weren't really hiding under the bed—they discovered a safe there. 2. The cow probably didn't know how to use an ax—it injured a farmer who was holding one. 3. The headline writer wasn't urging readers to munch on kids—the story was about kids fixing healthful snacks. 4. Yep, it's about doctors who treat feet, not gigantic doctors. 5. Not a talking car, a talk about cars . . . 6. A clever detecting tree? Nope—just a painting found near a tree.

Collect Milo & Jazz's first five mysteries!

★The Case of the Stinky Socks
Booklist, starred review
Book Links' Best New Books for the Classroom
Detective duo Milo and Jazz have to find the sock thief—before the big game!

The Case of the Poisoned Pig
Can Milo and Jazz catch the mysterious pig poisoner? "Highly recommended." —*Midwest Book Review*

The Case of the *Haunted* Haunted House
Milo and Jazz must find out if their class's "haunted house" is really haunted! "Builds up to an exciting finish."
—*Mysterious Reviews*

The Case of the Amazing Zelda
Is the pet psychic truly as amazing as she seems? Milo and Jazz are on the case! "Fun page-turner." —*Library Media Connection*

The Case the July 4th Jinx
Is the fair jinxed . . . or is it a case of *sabotage*? "Excellent summer reading."
—*Midwest Book Review*

COMING SOON
Book 7: The Case of the Purple Pool
And more mysteries from your favorite detectives (in training)!

Be sure to check out www.kanepress.com for other series from The Kane Press.

ABOUT THE AUTHOR

Lewis B. Montgomery is the pen name of a writer whose favorite authors include CSL, EBW, and LMM. Those initials are a clue—but there's another clue, too. Can you figure out their names?

Besides writing the Milo & Jazz mysteries, LBM enjoys eating spicy Thai noodles and blueberry ice cream, riding a bike, and reading. Not all at the same time, of course. At least, not anymore. But that's another story. . . .

ABOUT THE ILLUSTRATOR

Amy Wummer has illustrated more than 50 children's books. She uses pencils, watercolors, and ink—but not the invisible kind.

Amy and her husband, who is also an artist, live in Pennsylvania . . . in a mysterious old house which has a secret hidden room in the basement!